Tips for Reading Together

Children learn best when reading is fun.

- Talk about the title and the pictures on the cover.
- Look through the pictures together and discuss what you think the story might be about.
- Read the story together, pointing to the words and inviting your child to join in.
- Give lots of praise as your child reads with you, and help them when necessary.
- Have fun finding the hidden ladybirds.
- Enjoy re-reading the story and encourage your child to say the repeated phrases with you.

Children enjoy reading stories again and again.
This helps to build their confidence.

Have fun!

Find the ladybird hidden in every picture.

Poor Old Rabbit!

Written by Cynthia Rider
Illustrated by Alex Brychta

OXFORD
UNIVERSITY PRESS

Floppy saw a toy rabbit.

"Poor old rabbit,"
said Floppy.

"Nobody wants it."

Floppy took it to Kipper.

"Poor old rabbit,"
said Kipper.

Kipper took it to Mum.

"Look at this rabbit,"
said Kipper.

"Nobody wants it."

"Poor old rabbit," said Mum.

Dad washed it.

Kipper brushed it.

Chip and Wilma mended it.

Everybody wanted it now.

Oh no!

"Poor old rabbit,"
said Kipper.

Think about the story

Why do you think somebody has put the rabbit in the bin?

Why isn't it always safe to take toys out of the bin in the park?

Why did everybody want the rabbit at the end of the story?

What is your favourite toy? What would you do if it got old and torn?

A maze

Help Kipper to get to the rabbit.

More books for you to enjoy

Level 1: Getting Ready

Level 2: Starting to Read

Level 3: Becoming a Reader

Level 4: Building Confidence

Level 5: Reading with Confidence

OXFORD
UNIVERSITY PRESS

Great Clarendon Street,
Oxford OX2 6DP

British Library Cataloguing
in Publication Data available

ISBN 978-0-19-838557-8

10 9 8 7 6 5 4

Printed in China by Imago

Have more fun with Read at Home

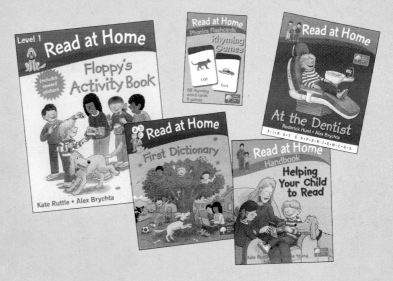